# Holly's Christmas Eve

## Wendy Watson

HarperCollins Publishers

It was Christmas Eve, and getting dark.
In the living room
electric candles glowed softly at the windows.
A fir tree stood tall in a corner,
covered with sparkling decorations
of all shapes and colors.
Murmuring voices filled the air—
the ornaments were talking.

"Toot, toot!" said Train Engine.

"Who's new?"

"I'm new!" said a little painted wood ornament.

"My name is Wooden Doll, but I call myself Holly."

She curtsied.

"Welcome!" said Train Engine.

"Glad to meet you, *señorita!*" said Tin Horse.

"Greetings, little one," said Cloth Bear.

Before anyone else could speak,

the whole tree began to shake.

"It's Bad Cat!" said Train Engine.

"Bad Cat?" asked Holly.

She heard scratchings and scrabblings

and shatterings of glass—

*pop, pop, pop, pop!*

Bad Cat was knocking ornaments to the floor

as he scrambled up the tree.

"Now he's coming after me!" said Holly.

Bad Cat swatted her,

up and down, this way and that,

until—*crick-crick-crack*—

Holly's left arm broke off

and tumbled down through the branches.

"Oh, no, no!" cried Cloth Bear.

A door opened, and footsteps hurried in.

"Bad Cat!" a voice shouted.

"Look what you've done!"

Bad Cat leapt off the tree and darted away.

A roaring monster rushed into the room.

"It's Vacuum Cleaner!" said Train Engine.

As Holly stared,

Vacuum Cleaner gobbled up

shattered glass, ornament holders,

fir needles . . .

and her arm!

Then Vacuum Cleaner went away,

and the roaring stopped.

Holly burst into tears.

"My poor arm!" she cried.

"I'll help you find it," said Tin Horse.

"So will I," said Cloth Bear.

"Cheer up! Cheer up!" whistled Train Engine.

"Almost time to celebrate!"

"Not yet!" cried Holly.

She brushed the tears from her eyes.

Then she and Cloth Bear and Tin Horse

bumped and slid all the way to the bottom of the tree

and stepped onto the floor.

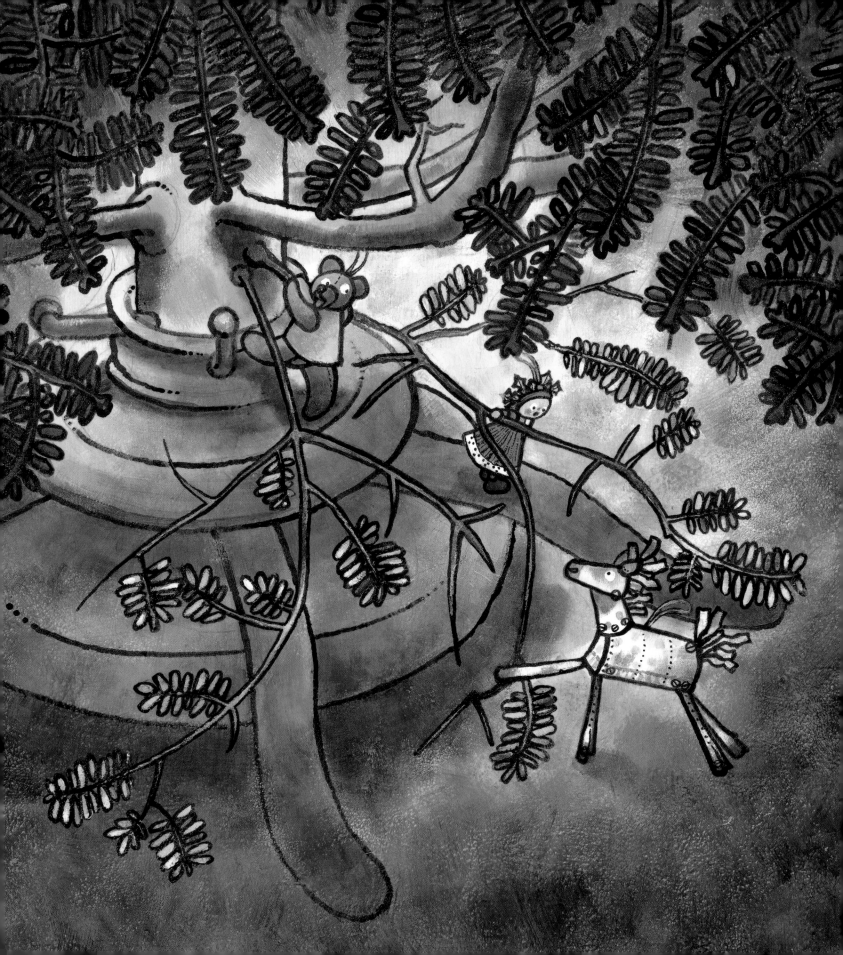

Out of the living room, into the hall . . .

the three ornaments skidded and skated

across the slippery floor.

Suddenly a furry creature scuttled toward them.

"Aha," chortled Spider. "I'll take this one!"

In a flash he lassoed Holly.

"Stop!" shouted Tin Horse.

He and Cloth Bear yanked Holly this way and that

until she was free.

Down the hall they all ran.

Where was Vacuum Cleaner?

"Ha, ha! Over here!" a voice suddenly growled.

The ornaments jumped and looked behind them.

"Vacuum Cleaner!" Holly curtsied.

"We're looking for—for my arm."

"Ha!" growled Vacuum Cleaner.

His cord quivered and swayed.

"First guess this!

Tall, fragrant, always green,

Proud I be, the forest queen."

"It's Fir Tree," said Holly. "But where is my arm now?"

"Ha, ha!" growled Vacuum Cleaner.

"Guess again!

Big round belly, small round feet,

A lion's roar, loves to eat!"

"That's you—Vacuum Cleaner!" said Cloth Bear.

"You have the arm!"

"Not anymore!" snarled Vacuum Cleaner.

"Guess this one!

*What none desire*

*Yet all acquire.*"

"Trash!" said Tin Horse. "Is it Trash?"

"Ha, ha, ha!" roared Vacuum Cleaner.

"Trash! Go look in Trash Can—

if you can get away!"

Vacuum Cleaner lunged toward them,

but they dashed out of his reach.

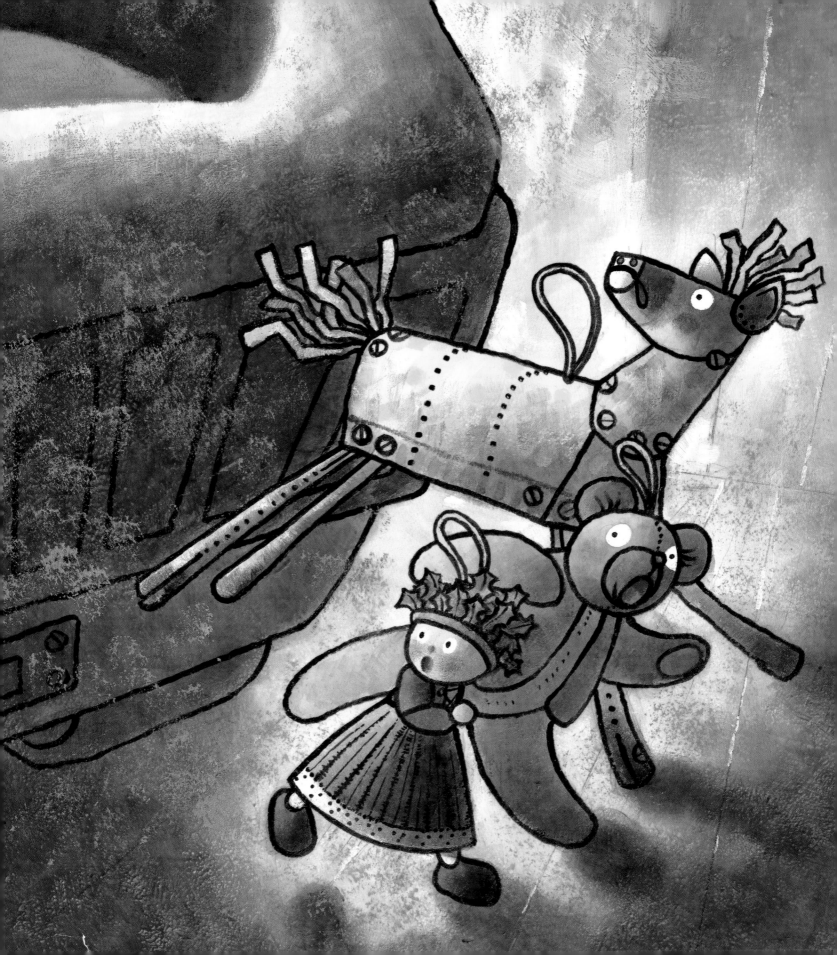

Racing around a corner,

the three ornaments ran straight into Trash Can!

Huffing and puffing, they struggled

right to the top,

and there they found Vacuum Cleaner's old bag.

"I'm too scared to go in there," said Cloth Bear.

"So am I," said Tin Horse.

"I'm not," said Holly,

and she climbed headfirst into the bag.

Holly dug through crumbs and sugars and flours.
She picked through needles
and lost buttons and pins.
She waded through bits of glass ornaments
and fir needles and sequins.
Then Holly saw something. . . .
"I think . . . I think . . .
Yes! It's my arm!" she cried.
She crawled back to the bag's opening,
clutching her broken arm.

"You've found it!" shouted Cloth Bear and Tin Horse.
As Holly squeezed out of the bag,
they heard the *ringle-jingle*,
*ringle-jingle* of sleigh bells.
"Hurry—hop on my back!" said Tin Horse.
With Holly and Cloth Bear holding tight,
Tin Horse scrambled to the floor and raced—
*clackety-clickety-clack, clackety-clickety-clack*—
all the way back to the living room.

"There's Bad Cat!" said Holly.

"*Carumba!*" said Tin Horse. "Let's charge him!"

"Not now, for heaven's sake!" said Cloth Bear.

"Attention!" Train Engine tooted from the tree.

"Here comes Santa!"

The ornaments cheered.

"Whiskers and whistles." Santa Claus chuckled.
"I have surprises for you.
Shut your eyes!"
Holly felt Santa tipping her over . . .
touching her shoulder . . .
hanging her back on the tree.
She heard Santa Claus rustling and rummaging
and ornaments whispering and giggling.
Finally Santa Claus spoke again.
"You can look now!" he said.

Holly opened her eyes.

"Santa Claus!" she said. "You fixed my arm! Thank you!"

"I love this new bow," said Cloth Bear.

"And my hat is *magnifico!*" said Tin Horse.

Just then a clock began to strike the hour.

"Sleigh bells and snowflakes," said Santa Claus. "It's time for me to leave!"

"Good-bye, Santa!" cried the ornaments.

"Good-bye, good-bye," said Santa Claus, "and a Merry Christmas to all!"

Then he was gone.

"Now," said Train Engine, "now we can celebrate!"

It was Christmas Eve, and the night was dark.
In the living room
electric candles glowed softly at the windows.
A fir tree stood tall in a corner,
covered with sparkling decorations
of all shapes and colors.
Laughter and music filled the room—
the ornaments were singing!
But not all of them. . . .
In the midst of the excitement,
three tired friends snuggled close together
and smiled as they slept.

For all of you

Holly's Christmas Eve
Copyright © 2002 by Wendy Watson
Printed in Hong Kong. All rights reserved.
www.harperchildrens.com
Library of Congress Cataloging-in-Publication Data    Watson, Wendy.
Holly's Christmas Eve / Wendy Watson.    p.      cm.
Summary: Before Santa Claus arrives on Christmas Eve, two tree ornaments help another one recover
her wooden arm after it is knocked off by a tree-climbing cat and then swept up by the vacuum cleaner.
ISBN 0-688-17652-6     ISBN 0-688-17653-4 (library binding)
[1. Christmas decorations—Fiction.    2. Christmas—Fiction.    3. Vacuum cleaners—Fiction.
4. Friendship—Fiction.    5. Santa Claus—Fiction.]    I. Title.
PZ7.W332 Ho    2002    2001039514    [E]—dc21
Typography by Carla Weise
1  2  3  4  5  6  7  8  9  10
❖
First Edition